DREAMWORKS

HOW TO TRAIN YOUR
DRAGON 2

Dragon Mountain
Adventure

adapted by Judy Katschke

illustrated by Justin Gerard
and Charles Grosvenor

Ready-to-Read

Simon Spotlight

New York   London   Toronto   Sydney   New Delhi

D0206533

SIMON SPOTLIGHT

An imprint of Simon & Schuster Children's Publishing Division

1230 Avenue of the Americas, New York, New York 10020

How To Train Your Dragon 2 © 2014 Dreamworks Animation, L.L.C.

For information about special discounts for bulk purchases,

please contact Simon & Schuster Special Sales at 1-866-506-1949 or business@simonandschuster.com.

The Simon & Schuster Speakers Bureau can bring authors to your live event.

For more information or to book an event contact the Simon & Schuster Speakers Bureau

at 1-866-248-3049 or visit our website at www.simonspeakers.com.

Manufactured in the United States of America 0614 LAK

4 6 8 10 9 7 5

ISBN 978-1-4814-0440-2 (pbk)

ISBN 978-1-4814-0441-9 (hc)

ISBN 978-1-4814-0442-6 (eBook)

Hiccup knew all about dragons.
He knew they weren't all fierce,
and that some made good friends.
How did he know?
Hiccup's best friend was a dragon,
and his name was Toothless!

Hiccup once dreamed
of being a dragon slayer.
He once even shot down a Night Fury!
Hiccup tried to slay the dragon
but could not.
Instead he built a harness
to help the injured dragon fly.

Now each time Toothless flew,
he flew with Hiccup!

Hiccup and Toothless were a team.
One day as they flew over icebergs,
they met a strange dragon and rider.
The rider captured Hiccup and took
him to a mountain hideaway.
Toothless sank down to the cold sea!

Hiccup asked many questions, but the masked rider stayed silent. Hiccup followed the rider into a dark chamber. There were more dragons there. Toothless arrived too! The dragons had saved him!

The rider touched a dragon
with a staff. It was a signal
to the dragons to shine fire
from their throats.
Hiccup and Toothless glowed
in the firelight. Hiccup didn't
understand. What was going on?

"Do I know you?"
Hiccup asked. The rider
took off the mask. It was a woman!
"A mother never forgets,"
she said gently.
Hiccup was stunned.
His mother Valka had been missing
for many years.

"Where have you been?" Hiccup asked. "Everyone thinks you were eaten by dragons!"

Valka led Hiccup to a secret cave.
The cave was filled with dragons.
They were all sizes and breeds,
and some were hurt.

When Hiccup saw the dragons,
he understood.
His mom wasn't eaten by dragons.
His mom had been rescuing dragons!

A few curious dragons
sniffed at Toothless.
But there was one special dragon
Valka wanted Hiccup to meet!

Valka pointed down to the bottom
of an underground cliff.
Sleeping on the bank was the
great Bewilderbeast!
"This is king of all dragons,"
Valka declared.
He was the alpha dragon,
which made him the boss!

"We all live under his care
and command," Valka explained.
"All but the hatchlings."
Hiccup smiled as baby dragons
hopped on the alpha's back.
The Bewilderbeast didn't roar.
He was cool. As cool as the
ice he snorted on Hiccup!

Valka and Hiccup took
to the sky on their dragons!
Hiccup didn't feel the frosty air.
All he felt was free!
Even the dragons had fun
battling for sky space!
Show-offs!

Now it was Hiccup's turn to show off.
"Can you fly?" Hiccup called to his
mom. He leaped off Toothless
into the sky.
Valka couldn't believe her eyes.
Hiccup was flying like a dragon!

Suddenly a fancy move hurled
Hiccup toward an icy cliff!
Toothless raced to grab Hiccup,
but he couldn't turn sharp enough.
What came next was a midair
pileup and a snowy crash landing!

Next Valka taught Hiccup
everything she knew about
dragons.
Hiccup watched as his mom
touched Toothless's back fins.
They split like magic!
"Every dragon has its secrets,"
Valka said. "Now you can
make those tight turns."

Valka had a secret too.

She wanted to rescue
the dragons of Berk!
Hiccup didn't understand.
The dragons in his village were well
and happy!
"But they're not safe," Valka said.
"Drago is coming for
all the dragons."

Hiccup knew about Drago,
the terrible dragon thief.
It wasn't long before
Valka's warnings came true.
Drago and his army
invaded Dragon Mountain!
But Valka had an army of dragons, too.
She also had the Bewilderbeast.

Drago came with a secret weapon.
He had his own Bewilderbeast,
trained to be wicked like himself!
Everyone watched as the
alphas faced off.
Valka's dragon put up a
good fight until a powerful swipe
brought him down!

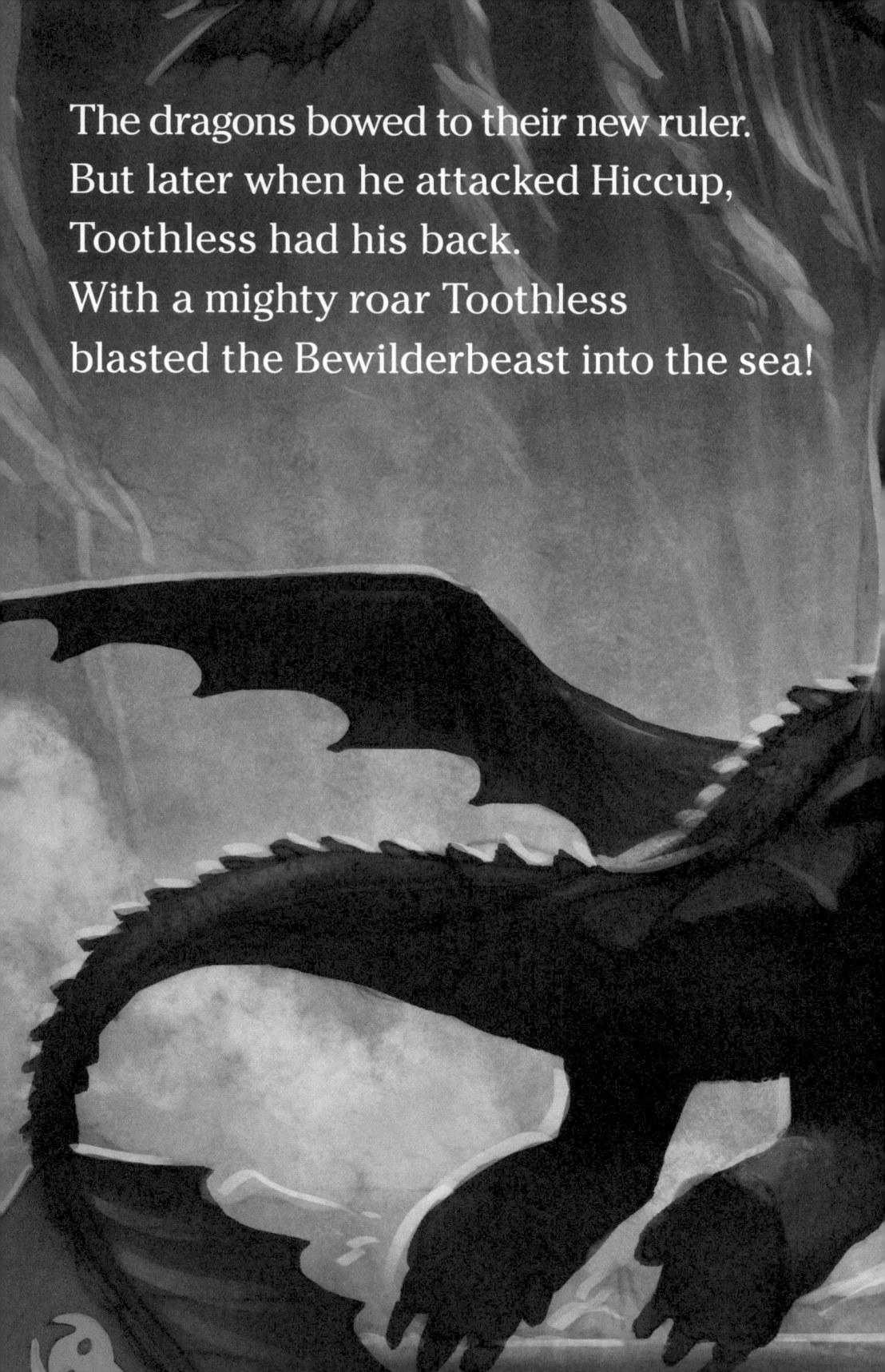

The dragons bowed to their new ruler.
But later when he attacked Hiccup,
Toothless had his back.
With a mighty roar Toothless
blasted the Bewilderbeast into the sea!

The new alpha dragon was not a
Bewilderbeast. It was a gentle,
but powerful Night Fury.
His name was Toothless!